Will Moses
MOTHER GOOSE

Philomel Books 🍎 New York

PATRICIA LEE GAUCH, EDITOR

Designed by Semadar Megged.
Text set in 17-point Cheltenham Light.
The art was done in oil on Fabriano paper.

Library of Congress Cataloging-in-Publication Data
Moses, Will.
Will Moses Mother Goose / Will Moses.
p. cm.   Summary: Folk art paintings accompany this
compilation of over sixty of the best-loved Mother Goose rhymes.
1. Nursery rhymes. 2. Children's poetry. [1. Nursery rhymes.]
I. Title. PZ8.3.M8436 Wi 2003   398.8—dc21   2003000731

ISBN 0-399-23744-5
3 5 7 9 10 8 6 4

WILL MOSES ON MOTHER GOOSE

I fondly remember being read to as a child, and more often than not, it seems that I remember the Mother Goose rhymes best. At bedtime, before our old and familiar stone fireplace hearth, still sparking and flickering with glowing embers, my mother would read these cherished rhymes. Humpty Dumpty, Peter Peter Pumpkin Eater, and The Old Woman Who Lived in a Shoe were favorites of mine. I remember thinking what a tragedy it was for an egg who could, presumably, dress himself and climb a wall to end it in a clumsy fall. And thinking, too, what an odd fellow that Peter is. And that the real story of the old woman who lived in a shoe was not the woman and her children, but rather, who wore the shoe before they lived in it? Where is he now? And how big he must have been!

I have forgotten which version of Mother Goose we had at home, but over the years, I have often thought how interesting and fun it would be to illustrate some of those rhymes and riddles I recall from my childhood days. A few years ago, after I came across a tattered old book called *The Boys and Girls Mother Goose*, I found myself thinking more and more about the possibility of doing a nursery rhyme book. I started thinking about how my art would translate into the world of Mother Goose and wondered if my paintings would make a new version worthwhile.

Now, those of you who have followed my work over the years may view this book as something of an artistic and literary departure for me, and I don't disagree. However, for some time, I have noticed that some of my best and most loyal fans are little people. Children have always found something fascinating in the subjects, color, detail, and stories that I try to convey with my paintings. So, while I hope both adults and children will enjoy this book, I have created it for little folks. And with luck, maybe this version of Mother Goose will be the one affectionately recalled by our children, years from now.

Will Moses

To Sharon, Mother Goose to our kids!

MOTHER GOOSE

Little Bo-Peep has lost her sheep,
And can't tell where to find them;
Leave them alone, and they'll come home,
Wagging their tails behind them.

Goosey, goosey gander,
Whither dost thou wander?
Up stairs and down stairs,
And in my lady's chamber.

As I was going to St. Ives
I met a man with seven wives;
Each wife had seven sacks,
In each sack were seven cats,
And each cat had seven kits.
Kits, cats, sacks, and wives,
How many were going to St. Ives?

Three wise men of Gotham
Went to sea in a bowl.
If the bowl had been stronger,
My song would have been longer.

Humpty Dumpty sat on a wall,
Humpty Dumpty had a great fall;
All the King's horses and all the King's men
Couldn't put Humpty together again.

An apple pie, when it looks nice,
Would make one long to have a slice,
But if the taste should prove so, too,
I fear one slice would scarcely do.
So to prevent my asking twice,
Pray, Mamma, cut a good large slice.

Mary had a little lamb,
Its fleece was white as snow;
And everywhere that Mary went
The lamb was sure to go.
It followed her to school one day,
It was against the rule,
And made the children laugh and play
To see a lamb at school.

Handy Pandy, Jack-a-dandy,
Loves plum cake and sugar candy.
He bought some at a grocer's shop
And out he came, hop, hop, hop!

I had a little hen, the prettiest ever seen;
She washed me the dishes and kept the house clean;
She went to the mill to fetch me some flour,
She brought it home in less than an hour;
She baked me my bread, she brewed me my ale,
She sat by the fire and told many a fine tale.

There was an old soldier of Bister
Who went walking one day with his sister,
When a cow at one poke
Tossed her into an oak,
Before the old gentleman missed her.

To market, to market, to buy a fat pig,
Home again, home again, jiggety jig.
To market, to market, to buy a fat hog,
Home again, home again, jiggety jog.

There was a crooked man,
        and he went a crooked mile;
He found a crooked sixpence
        against a crooked stile;
He bought a crooked cat,
        which caught a crooked mouse;
And they all lived together
        in a little crooked house.

Diddle diddle dumpling, my son John,
Went to bed with his breeches on,
One stocking off, and one stocking on,
Diddle diddle dumpling, my son John.

Hickory, dickory, dock;
The mouse ran up the clock.
The clock struck one,
The mouse ran down,
Hickory, dickory, dock.

Pussy-cat, pussy-cat, where have you been?
I've been up to London to look at the queen.
Pussy-cat, pussy-cat, what did you there?
I frightened a little mouse under her chair.

"**W**ill you walk into my parlour?"
    said the spider to the fly.
"'Tis the prettiest little parlour
    that ever you did spy.
The way into my parlour
    is up a winding stair;
And I have many curious things
    to show you when you're there."
"Oh, no, no," said the little fly,
    "to ask me is in vain;
For who goes up your winding stair
    can ne'er come down again."

Jack Sprat could eat no fat,
His wife could eat no lean,
And so between them both,
They licked the platter clean.

Jack ate all the lean,
Joan ate all the fat;
The bone they picked clean,
Then gave it to the cat.

Mary, Mary, quite contrary,
How does your garden grow?
With silver bells and cockleshells
And pretty maids all in a row.

The fair maid who, the first of May,
Goes to the fields at break of day,
And washes in dew from the hawthorn tree,
Will ever after handsome be.

Three little kittens,
They lost their mittens,
And they began to cry.
Oh, Mother dear,
We sadly fear,
Our mittens we have lost.
What! Lost your mittens,
You naughty kittens!
Then you shall have no pie.
Meow, meow, meow.
You shall have no pie.

Willy boy, Willy boy, where are you going?
I will go with you, if that I may.
I'm going to the meadow to see them a-mowing,
I'm going to help them make the hay.

If wishes were horses,
   Beggars would ride;
   If turnips were watches,
   I would wear one by my side.

The man in the wilderness asked me,
   How many strawberries grew in
      the sea?
I answered him, as I thought good,
As many as red herrings grew
      in the wood.

There was an old woman tossed up in a basket,
Seventy times high as the moon.
What she did there I could not but ask it,
For in her hand she carried a broom.
"Old woman, old woman, old woman," said I,
"Oh whither, oh whither, oh whither so high?"
"To sweep the cobwebs off from the sky,
And I shall be back again by and by."

Wee Willie Winkie runs through the town,
Upstairs and downstairs, in his nightgown;
Rapping at the window, crying through the lock,
"Are the children in their beds? Now it's eight o'clock."

The man in the moon came down too soon
And asked the way to Norwich;
He went by the south and burnt his mouth
Eating cold plum-porridge.

Twinkle, twinkle, little star,
How I wonder what you are,
Up above the world so high,
Like a diamond in the sky.

As your bright and tiny spark
Lights the traveller in the dark,
Though I know not what you are,
Twinkle, twinkle, little star.

Little boy blue, go blow your horn;
The sheep's in the meadow, the cow's in the corn.
Where's the little boy that tends the sheep?
He's under the haystack, fast asleep.

Robert Roley rolled a round
    roll round,
A round roll Robert Roley rolled
    round;
Where rolled the round roll
    Robert Roley rolled round?

Ring-a-ring-a-roses,
A pocket full of posies,
Hush-hush-hush,
We'll all tumble down.

A long-tailed pig or a short-tailed pig,
Or a pig without any tail.
A sow pig or a boar big,
Or a pig with a curly tail.

Charley Warley had a cow
Black and white about the brow;
Open the gate and let her go through,
Charley Warley's old cow!

Donkey, donkey, old and gray,
Open your mouth to gently bray;
Lift your ears and blow your horn,
To wake the world this sleepy morn.

When the wind is in the east,
'Tis good for neither man nor beast;
When the wind is in the north,
The skillful fisher goes not forth;
When the wind is in the south,
It blows the bait in the fishes' mouth;
When the wind is in the west,
Then 'tis at the very best.

Doctor Foster went to Glo'ster,
In a shower of rain;
He stepped in a puddle,
Up to his middle,
And never went there again.

It's raining, it's pouring,
The old man is snoring.
He went to bed and bumped his head
And couldn't get up in the morning.

Blow, wind, blow! And go, mill, go!
  That the miller may grind his corn;
  That the baker may take it,
  And into rolls make it,
  And send us some hot in the morn.

One misty, moisty morning,
  When cloudy was the weather,
  I chanced to meet an old man
  Clothed all in leather.

  He began to compliment,
  And I began to grin;
  How do you do, and how do you do?
  And how do you do again?

35

A thatcher of Thatchwood went to Thatchet a-thatching;
  Did a thatcher of Thatchwood go to Thatchet a-thatching?
  If a thatcher of Thatchwood went to Thatchet a-thatching,
  Where's the thatching the thatcher of Thatchwood thatched?

Birds of a feather flock together,
And so will pigs and swine;
Rats and mice will have their choice,
And so will I have mine.

Tom, Tom, the piper's son,
He learned to play when he was young,
But all the tune that he could play,
Was "Over the hills and far away."
Over the hills, and a great way off,
And the wind will blow my top-knot off.
Now Tom with his pipe made such a noise,
That he pleased both the girls and boys.

Upon my word of honor,
As I went to Bonner,
I met a pig
Without a wig
Upon my word and honor.

Baa, baa, black sheep,
Have you any wool?
Yes, sir, yes, sir,
Three bags full:
One for the master,
And one for the dame,
And one for the little boy
Who lives down the lane.

Jack and Jill went up the hill,
To fetch a pail of water;
Jack fell down and broke his crown,
And Jill came tumbling after.

The old woman must stand at the tub, tub, tub,
The dirty clothes to rub, rub, rub;
But when they are clean, and fit to be seen,
She'll dress like a lady, and dance on the green.

O
ld Mother Hubbard
Went to the cupboard
To give her poor dog a bone;
But when she came there,
Her cupboard was bare,
And so the poor dog had none.

H
ere's Sulky Sue;
What shall we do?
Turn her face to the wall
Till she comes to.

T
hree blind mice, see how they run!
They all ran after the farmer's wife,
Who cut off their tails with a carving knife.
Did you ever see such a sight in your life,
As three blind mice?

There was a little girl
And she had a little curl,
Right in the middle of her forehead;
And when she was good,
She was very, very good—
But when she was bad, she was horrid!

Here we go round the mulberry bush,
The mulberry bush, the mulberry bush.
Here we go round the mulberry bush,
On a cold and frosty morning.

Little Jack Horner sat in a corner
Eating his Christmas pie.
He put in his thumb
And pulled out a plum
And said, "What a good boy am I!"

Hey, rub-a-dub-dub, three men in a tub,
And who do you think were there?
The butcher, the baker, the candlestick maker,
And all had come from the fair.

The Queen of Hearts,
  She made some tarts,
  All on a summer's day;
The Knave of Hearts,
  He stole those tarts,
  And took them clean away.
The King of Hearts
  Called for the tarts,
  And beat the Knave full sore;
The Knave of Hearts
  Brought back the tarts,
  And vowed he'd steal no more.

Dickery, dickery, dare,
  The pig flew up in the air;
  The man in brown
  Soon brought him down,
  Dickery, dickery, dare.

Georgey Porgey, pudding and pie,
Kissed the girls and made them cry;
When the girls came out to play,
Georgey Porgey ran away.

Peter, Peter, pumpkin eater,
Had a wife and couldn't keep her.
He put her in a pumpkin shell,
And there he kept her very well.
Peter, Peter, pumpkin eater,
Had another and didn't love her.
Peter learned to read and spell,
And then he loved her very well.

There was an old woman
Lived under a hill,
And if she's not gone,
She lives there still.

There was an old woman
Who lived in a shoe;
She had so many children,
She didn't know what to do.
She gave them some broth,
Without any bread,
She whipped them all round,
And sent them to bed.

The kettle's on the fire
And we'll all have tea,
We'll also have a dumpling,
But nothing else there'll be.
A cup of tea that's piping hot,
Is just the thing to hit the spot.

Peter Piper picked a peck of pickled peppers;
A peck of pickled peppers Peter Piper picked.
If Peter Piper picked a peck of pickled peppers,
Where's the peck of pickled peppers Peter Piper picked?

Little Miss Muffet sat on a tuffet
Eating her curds and whey;
Along came a spider and sat down beside her,
And frightened Miss Muffet away.

Tweedle-dum and Tweedle-dee
Resolved to have a battle;
For Tweedle-dum said Tweedle-dee
Had spoiled his nice new rattle.
Just then flew by a monstrous crow,
As big as a tar barrel,
Which frightened both the heroes so,
They quite forgot their quarrel.

Barber, barber, shave a pig,
How many hairs will make a wig?
"Four and twenty, that's enough,"
Give the barber a pinch of snuff.

Up hill spare me,
Down hill ware me,
On level ground spare me not,
And in the stable forget me not.

a horse

As I went through the garden gap
Who should I meet but Dick Redcap!
A stick in his hand, a stone in his throat:
If you'll tell me this riddle
I'll give you a groat.

a cherry

If a man carried my burden
He would surely break his back.
I am not rich but always leave
Silver in my track.

a snail

As I went over Lincoln Bridge
I met Mister Rusticap;
Pins and needles on his back,
A-going to Thorney Fair.

a hedgehog

54

Hick-a-more, Hack-a-more,
On the King's kitchen door;
All the King's horses,
And all the King's men,
Couldn't drive Hick-a-more, Hack-a-more,
Off the King's kitchen door.

sunshine

As round as an apple
As deep as a cup
And all the King's horses
Can't pull it up.

a well

55

In marble walls as white as milk,
Lined with a skin as soft as silk;
Within a fountain crystal clear,
A golden apple doth appear.
No doors there are to this stronghold,
Yet thieves break in and steal the gold.

an egg

JUST WHO *WAS* MOTHER GOOSE?

The truth is, no one knows for sure. Some have traced the name Mother Goose all the way back to 1650, to Loret's *La Muse Historique*, which carried the subtitle *Comme un conte de la Mere Oye*, which means "Like a Mother Goose story." The Mother Goose part of the title has been linked to Queen Goosefoot, the legendary French storyteller and queen who was a patron of children. (She was called Goosefoot because of the size and shape of her feet!) Others claim an American origin in *Mother Goose's Melodies*, published in 1719 in Boston by Thomas Fleet, whose mother-in-law was Elizabeth Vergoose. But there is no way to be certain if either of these is how Mother Goose came to be.

We do know that in 1697, Charles Perrault used the phrase in a published collection of eight fairy tales, which included "Cinderella," "The Sleeping Beauty," and "Little Red Riding Hood." Although the book was titled *Histories and Tales of Long Ago, with Morals*, the frontispiece featured an old woman spinning and telling stories to children, and a placard bearing the words *Contes de la Mere l'Oye* ("Tales of My Mother the Goose").

But the Mother Goose we know now is more associated with children's rhymes than fairy tales. Many trace this change to John Newbery, for whom the Newbery Medal is named. He adopted the name Mother Goose for a collection of traditional rhymes, published somewhere between 1760 and 1766. This slim volume, *Mother Goose's Melody: or Sonnets for the Cradle*, edited by celebrated author Oliver Goldsmith, was an extraordinarily popular book among English-speaking children on both sides of the ocean.

Ever since, the Mother Goose tradition has been handed down, in folklore fashion, translated and retold in countries across the world. Will Moses, like so many before him, is passing down an age-old tradition, using his own imagination and distinct style to recreate a classic part of childhood. And we join children everywhere in being glad he did.

The Editors

BIBLIOGRAPHY FOR "JUST WHO *WAS* MOTHER GOOSE?"

Bett, Henry. *Nursery Rhymes and Tales: Their Origin and History.* London: Methuen & Co. Ltd., 1968.

Delamar, Gloria T. *Mother Goose, from Nursery to Literature.* Jefferson, N.C.: McFarland and Company, Inc., 1987.

Eckenstein, Lina. *Comparative Studies in Nursery Rhymes.* London: Duckworth & Co., 1906.

Opie, Iona A., and Peter Opie, eds. *The Oxford Dictionary of Nursery Rhymes.* New York: Oxford University Press, 1997.

INDEX OF FIRST LINES

61